The PiRaTe KoosToe

by Michael Scotto
illustrated by The Ink Circle

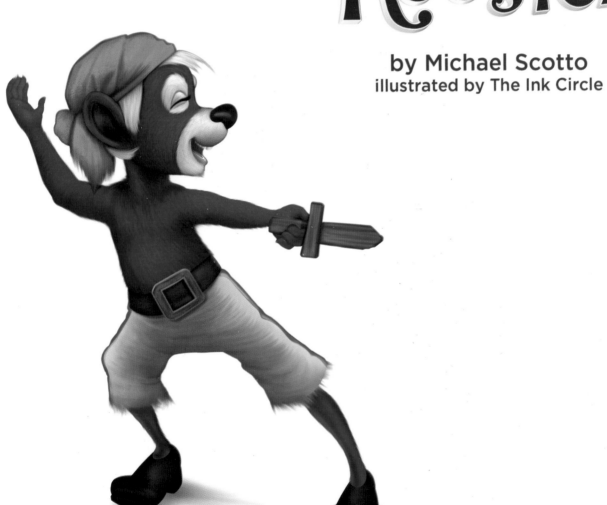

STARRING

LITTLE
KOOSTOE

Koostoe O. Bobo had a fascinating job. He was a ship captain. He loved to go exploring on the sea.

Even more, though,
Koostoe enjoyed sharing the
sea's treasures with others.

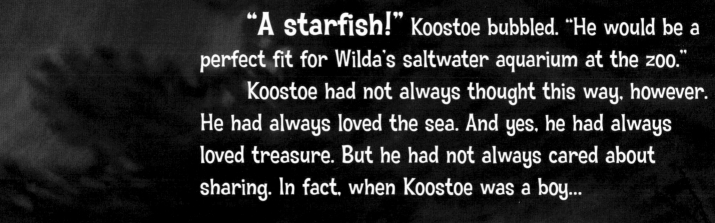

"A starfish!" Koostoe bubbled. "He would be a perfect fit for Wilda's saltwater aquarium at the zoo."

Koostoe had not always thought this way, however. He had always loved the sea. And yes, he had always loved treasure. But he had not always cared about sharing. In fact, when Koostoe was a boy...

"I want to be a pirate!" cried young Koostoe. He and some other Midlandians had been sharing what they wanted to be when they grew up.

"A pirate?" Nueva asked curiously. "What do pirates do?"

"Whatever they want!" declared Koostoe. "Pirates get to sail on the ocean all day long. But the best part about being a pirate is that it's your job to search for treasure!"

"I'm not so sure being a pirate is a good idea," said Dewey.

"Oh, really?" replied Koostoe with a smirk.

"I've read about pirates at the library," said Dewey. "They are not very nice. They get their treasure by taking it from others."

"That sounds like stealing to me," observed Nueva.

Koostoe felt himself becoming upset. "It's not stealing when you're a pirate!" he shouted. "You're just jealous because I found the perfect job! And I'm going to start working today. From now on, you will call me...**the pirate Koostoe!**"

Since he did not have a ship, Koostoe first tried to be a pirate on land. "Arrr!" he would growl, waving his little wooden sword. **"I am the pirate Koostoe!** Surrender your treasure!"

But nobody found him to be very convincing.

"What a darling costume!" raved Sew the seamstress.

"Your voice sounds funny," noted Doc Fixit. "Are you getting a cold?"

Koostoe began to grow sad,
and a little angry, too. "All I want
is to get some treasure," he sighed.
But then, Koostoe had an idea.

"A ship!" he exclaimed. "That's my
trouble. To be a real pirate, I need a ship.
And I know just the one...."

Every weekend, Chief Tatupu took his boat out to go
fishing. Chief worked hard as the leader of Midlandia, and
fishing helped him to relax.

"Such a perfectly peaceful day," he thought as he rowed.

Behind Chief, Koostoe sneaked up quietly on his little raft. As he paddled, though, the young pirate began to have doubts. "Maybe Nueva and Dewey were right," he thought. "This feels like stealing, and **stealing is wrong.**"

But then, Koostoe spotted something next to Chief in the boat. It was a wooden box with golden edges.
"Treasure!" cried Koostoe. So when he drew very close...

Koostoe jumped up and shouted, "Hold it right there, Chief! I claim that treasure chest for the pirate Koostoe. Hand it over or walk the plank!"

Chief saw the young Midlandian and chuckled. "Do you mean my tackle box?" he asked. "This is where I keep my hooks and bait. I am afraid that you cannot borrow it today."

"That's where you're wrong, matey!" growled Koostoe. **"Arrr!"**

Koostoe leapt high and landed in Chief's boat with a crack.

"Oh, dear," said Chief.
Koostoe's sword had poked a
hole in the boat!

Koostoe helped drag Chief's boat ashore. "I don't think I should be a pirate anymore," he said. "They're fun to read about, but I don't like trying to be mean, or stealing."

"I am glad to hear that," said Chief. "What made you want to be a pirate in the first place?"

"I like looking for treasure," explained Koostoe. "Plus, I really like sailing. That's another big part of being a pirate."

"There are other jobs where you could get to sail," remarked Chief. "Perhaps you should focus on one of those."

"But if I don't become a pirate," replied Koostoe, "how will I find any treasure?"

Chief simply replied, **"Treasure comes in many forms."**

Koostoe did not understand what Chief meant, but he decided to take his advice. Koostoe studied hard and worked at the docks. In time, he had saved enough money to build a small ship of his own.

Koostoe was quite proud of his ship, and he liked being its captain. "But I never found any treasure," he often thought.

One day, an old friend came to visit.
It was Dewey!

"Ever since I became the town librarian," he said, "I've been reading about the sea around Midlandia. I've learned a lot about it, but I've never had a chance to really be on the sea. Could you take me out on your ship?"

"Of course," replied Koostoe.

Koostoe sailed with Dewey all day. They saw
little islands nearby, schools of swimming fish, and
even a pod of dolphins. Koostoe enjoyed the trip...
"But it's no treasure hunt," he thought.

When they returned to the docks, Dewey shook Koostoe's hand. "Thank you!" said Dewey. "I will always treasure the memories from today."

Koostoe's ears perked up. "Treasure? Where?"

Dewey pointed to his heart. "The treasure is right in here," he said. "Today was one of the best days of my life. A day like this is more precious than gold or jewels."

Koostoe finally understood what Chief had meant. Treasure did not have to be buried in the sand. It could be anything that someone valued, like a happy memory, or the great feeling Koostoe got from helping his friend. Or even...

"A starfish!" cried
Wilda. "This will be perfect
for my saltwater aquarium."

"I just knew that you would like it," said Koostoe.
"Thank you so much, Koostoe!" said Wilda. "You are a real treasure."
To which Koostoe simply replied, "Treasure comes in many forms."

Discussion Questions

What sorts of hobbies or interests do you have?
Can you think of any jobs that involve your interests?

Name a person you admire. What does he or she do for a job?
What would you like to do for a job when you grow up?